Dear Dragon Goes to Grandpa's Farm

by Margaret Hillert

Illustrated by Jack Pullan

NORWOOD HOUSE PRESS

DEAR CAREGIVER, The *Beginning-to-Read* series is a carefully written collection of classic readers you may remember from your own childhood. Each book features text comprised of common sight words to provide your child ample practice reading the words that appear most frequently in written text. The many additional details in the pictures enhance the story and offer the opportunity for you to help your child expand oral language and develop comprehension.

Begin by reading the story to your child, followed by letting him or her read familiar words and soon your child will be able to read the story independently. At each step of the way, be sure to praise your reader's efforts to build his or her confidence as an independent reader. Discuss the pictures and encourage your child to make connections between the story and his or her own life. At the end of the story, you will find reading activities and a word list that will help your child practice and strengthen beginning reading skills.

Above all, the most important part of the reading experience is to have fun and enjoy it!

Shannon Cannon

Shannon Cannon, Ph.D.
Literacy Consultant

Norwood House Press • P.O. Box 316598 • Chicago, Illinois 60631
For more information about Norwood House Press please visit our website at
www.norwoodhousepress.com or call 866-565-2900.
Text copyright ©2015 by Margaret Hillert. Illustrations and cover design copyright ©2015
by Norwood House Press, Inc. All rights reserved. No part of this book may be reproduced
or utilized in any form or by any means without written permission from the publisher.

LIBRARY OF CONGRESS CATALOGING-IN-PUBLICATION DATA
Hillert, Margaret.
    Dear Dragon goes to grandpa's farm / by Margaret Hillert ; illustrated by Jack Pullan.
        pages cm. -- (A Beginning-to-read book)
    Summary: "A boy and his pet dragon visit Grandpa's farm. They see several farm
animals, even a blue pony! This title includes reading activities and a word list"--
Provided by publisher.
    ISBN 978-1-59953-675-0 (library edition : alk. paper) -- ISBN
978-1-60357-735-9 (ebook)
    [1. Farms--Fiction. 2. Dragons--Fiction.] I. Pullan, Jack. II. Title.
    PZ7.H558Deaj 2015
    [E]--dc23
                                    2014030281

262N—122014
Manufactured in the United States of America in North Mankato, Minnesota.

Come here. Come here.
I have something for you.
Something you will like.

What is it?

What is it?

What do you have for me?

Oh, I can read this.
But how funny!
Grandfather wants us to come to his farm.

He wants us to see his blue pony.
A blue pony?
How can we see a blue pony?
A pony is not blue!

Can we go?
Can we go?
We want to visit Grandfather.
We want to see the blue pony.
We want to see the farm.

Come with me.
You can all come with me.
Mother and the baby will stay here.

Away we go.
Away, away, away.
What fun this is.

Grandfather! Grandfather!
Here we are.
Where is the blue pony?
We want to see it.

13

You will see.
You will see.
But not now.

Run, run, run.
I want you to see
something first.

Look in here.
See what we have here?
One, two, three little ones.
Three little ones and a mother.

And look at this!
How do you like this big one?
So BIG!
So BIG!

And here are the mothers
with their eggs.

Soon the baby chicks will come out of the egg.

Here are some pretty babies.
Pretty yellow babies.

22

What a big baby this is!
It can run and jump.
It can play.

It is fun to look at things,
but where is the blue pony?
Can we see the blue pony now?

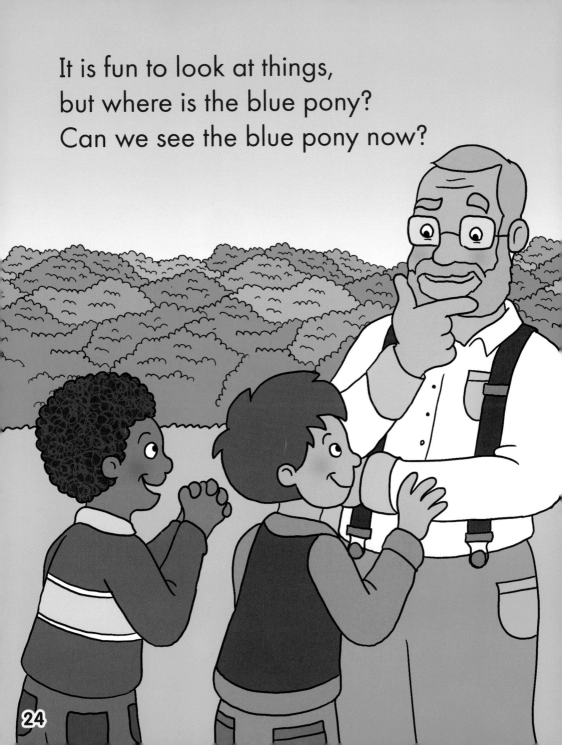

Yes. Yes.
The pony is in here.
Go in here.
Go in, go in.

Oh, look at this!
You do have a blue pony!
You do! You do!
It is so pretty!

Get up here with us, Dragon.
Now we can ride and ride and ride.
Here you are with me.
And here I am with you.
Oh what a happy day, Dear Dragon.

The following activities support the findings of the National Reading Panel that determined the most effective components for reading instruction are: Phonemic Awareness, Phonics, Vocabulary, Fluency, and Text Comprehension.

Phonemic Awareness: The /f/ and /v/ sounds

1. Say the word fine and ask your child to repeat the /**f**/ sound.

2. Say the word vine and ask your child to repeat the /**v**/ sound.

3. Explain to your child that you are going to say some words and you would like her/him to show you one finger if the sound in the word is /**f**/, as in fine or two fingers if the sound in the word is /**v**/, as in vine.

face	vase	farm	fork	fest
beef	move	leave	vent	fox
vine	vote	fast	elf	have
dive	fish	very	view	food
fun	love	leaf	roof	

Phonics: Consonants f and v

1. Demonstrate how to form the letters f and v for your child.

2. Have your child practice writing f and v at least three times each.

3. Divide a piece of paper in half by folding it the long way. Draw a line on the fold. Turn it so that the paper has two columns. Write the words fine and vine at the top of the columns.

4. Write the words above on separate index cards. Ask your child to sort the words based on the f and v spellings.

Word Work: Plurals

1. Explain to your child that when there is more than one of something it is a plural (for example: boy/boys, girl/girls, cloud/clouds, etc.).

2. Explain to your child that when words end in the **/f/** sound, and it is plural, the **/f/** sound becomes the **/v/** sound and **es** is added.

3. Write the following words in a list: leaf, elf, knife, life, loaf, scarf, wife, wolf.

4. Spell the word leaves next to the word leaf to demonstrate.

5. Ask your child to change the rest of the words to plurals (elves, knives, lives, loaves, scarves, wives, wolves).

Fluency: Echo Reading

1. Reread the story to your child at least two more times while your child tracks the print by running a finger under the words as they are read. Ask your child to read the words he or she knows with you.

2. Reread the story, stopping after each sentence or page to allow your child to read (echo) what you have read. Repeat echo reading and let your child take the lead.

Text Comprehension: Discussion Time

1. Ask your child to retell the sequence of events in the story.

2. To check comprehension, ask your child the following questions:

   • Where does Grandpa live?

   • What animals did he have?

   • Where was the blue pony?

   • Have you been on a farm? What animals did you see? If not, name some animals you might like to see.

Dear Dragon Goes to Grandpa's Farm uses the 81 words listed below.
The **5** words bolded below serve as an introduction to new vocabulary, while the other 76 are pre-primer. You may wish to write the words on index cards and use them to help your child build automatic word recognition. Regular practice with these words will enhance your child's fluency in reading connected text.

a	**egg(s)**	I	play	up
all		in	**pony**	us
am	farm	is	pretty	
and	first	it		
are	for		read	**visit**
at	fun	jump	ride	
away	funny		run	want(s)
		like		we
babies	get	little	see	what
baby	go	look	so	where
big	**Grandfather**		some	will
blue		me	something	with
but	happy	Mother(s)	soon	
	have		stay	yellow
can	he	not		yes
chicks	here	now	the	you
come	his		their	
	how	of	things	
day		oh	this	
dear		one(s)	three	
do		out	to	
Dragon			two	

ABOUT THE AUTHOR

Margaret Hillert has written over 80 books for children who are just learning to read. Her books have been translated into many different languages and over a million children throughout the world have read her books. She first started writing poetry as a child and has continued to write for children and adults throughout her life. A first grade teacher for 34 years, Margaret is now retired from teaching and lives in Michigan where she likes to write, take walks in the morning, and care for her three cats.

Photograph by Glenna Washburn

ABOUT THE ILLUSTRATOR

A talented and creative illustrator, Jack Pullan, is a graduate of William Jewell College. He has also studied informally at Oxford University and the Kansas City Art Institute. He was mentored by the renowned watercolor artists, Jim Hamil and Bill Amend. Jack's work has graced the pages of many enjoyable children's books, various educational materials, cartoon strips, as well as many greeting cards. Jack currently resides in Kansas.